Rabbit and Coyote

Retold from a Mayan legend
by Dawn McMillan
Illustrated by Kiera Poelsma

Chapter 1
Coyote Looks for Dinner

Coyote was asleep all afternoon.
When he woke up it was dark,
and he was very hungry.

"I hope I can find some dinner in the dark,"
he said to himself.
"I'm glad the moon is shining brightly tonight.
I should be able to see well enough
to find something to eat."

In the bright moonlight
Coyote crept along the banks of the river.

Coyote looked this way, and that way,
and then he saw a rabbit!

"Great!" he whispered, and he licked his lips.
"Rabbit is out late tonight,
and a rabbit dinner is just what I need!"

Rabbit sat up on his back legs.
He sniffed! He sniffed again!
"I'm in danger!" he thought, as he looked around.
"I can smell coyote!"

Quickly, Rabbit turned and ran!
Coyote could see Rabbit's white tail
flashing in the moonlight,
and he chased after him.
Faster and faster they went,
away from the river and into the forest!

Chapter 2

Closer and Closer

Rabbit could hear Coyote
getting closer and closer.
By now he was very tired.
He knew that if he kept running,
Coyote would catch him.

Just then Rabbit came to a pool
in the middle of the forest.
There, in the water,
he saw the reflection of the moon.

When Coyote reached the pool
he saw Rabbit sitting by the water.

"Dinner time!" Coyote shouted, and he jumped at Rabbit!

But Rabbit got away and ran quickly to the other side of the pool.

"Ah, Rabbit," laughed Coyote, "I'm coming around there to get you! You are too tired to run away from me, and you will make such a delicious dinner!"

"You are right, Mr Coyote!" called Rabbit. "I cannot run any more, but before you eat me would you like some cheese? Rabbit and cheese taste great together!"

"Cheese?" asked Coyote. "I do love cheese! Where can I find such a tasty treat?"

"Why, Mr Coyote," Rabbit said,
as he pointed to the moon's reflection,
"just look in the water.
See! There is a big round cheese
at the bottom of the pool."

"So there is," said Coyote.
"Now that looks delicious!
But *you* look delicious too, Rabbit,
and I think I'd like to eat you now!"

"Oh, do have the cheese first," said Rabbit.
"I will taste much better
after you have eaten the cheese."

Where is the Cheese?

Coyote stepped into the pool to get the cheese. "The water is too deep and I can't reach it," he said.

"Oh, just look at it," said Rabbit. "Such a huge cheese, round and yellow, right in the middle of the pond. You will have to swim out to get it."

Coyote swam into the middle of the pond. He swam around and around. "Where is it? I can't see it!" he cried.

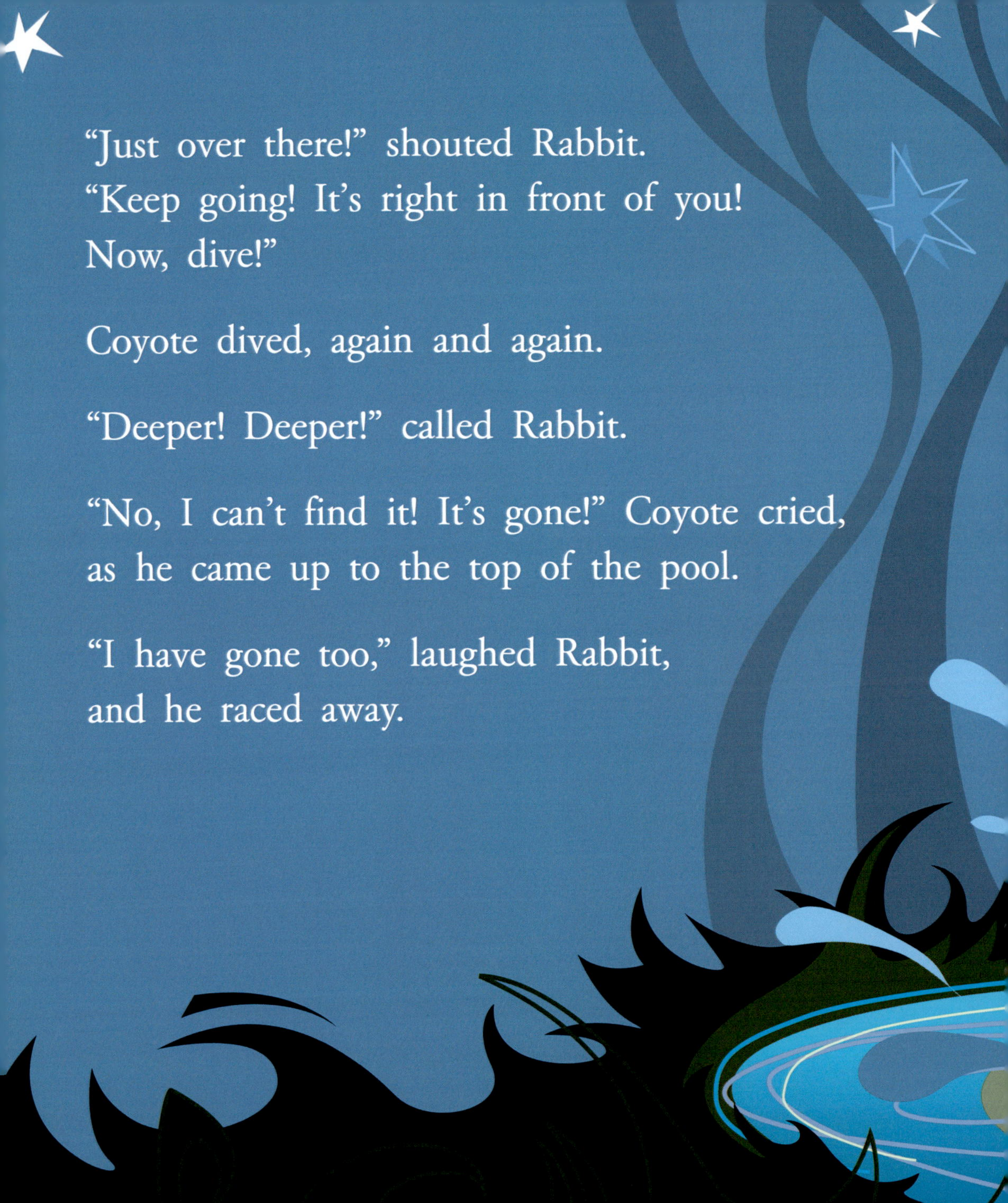

"Just over there!" shouted Rabbit.
"Keep going! It's right in front of you!
Now, dive!"

Coyote dived, again and again.

"Deeper! Deeper!" called Rabbit.

"No, I can't find it! It's gone!" Coyote cried, as he came up to the top of the pool.

"I have gone too," laughed Rabbit, and he raced away.

"Poor Coyote!" Rabbit called back.
"No cheese for dinner, and no rabbit!"